JEAN DE BRUNHOFF

BABAR

and

FATHER CHRISTMAS

METHUEN CHILDREN'S BOOKS

LONDON

"Oh, my friends!" said Zephir the little monkey one day to Arthur, Pom, Flora and Alexander, "listen to the wonderful story I have just been told. Every year, on Christmas Eve in the land of Men, a very kind old man with a long white beard and a red coat travels through the air. He carries many toys with him which he gives to the little children. He is called Father Christmas. It is difficult to see him, because he comes down the chimney while children are asleep. Next morning, they know that he has been because there are toys in their stockings. Why don't we write to him and ask him to come to the land of the elephants as well?"

"Oh, yes! What a good idea!" they all said.

They each decided which toys they
wanted and Zephir, who had the best
handwriting, wrote the letter. Arthur
remembered that they needed to stick a
stamp on the envelope. Then they all
signed the letter and went happily to
post it.

Every morning the five friends waited
for the postman to arrive.

But alas, there was no reply from Father Christmas.

One day Babar saw them looking so sad, and called them over. "Come now, children," he said, "what's the matter?"

Zephir told him all about the letter.
"Father Christmas can't have had time
to reply yet," said Babar. "Don't worry.
Go and play."

Then Babar walked up and down, thinking hard. "Why didn't I think of asking Father Christmas to come to the land of the elephants before?" he said to himself. "It would be best if I went to look for him. If I speak to him he will not refuse to come."

Babar decided to leave straight away. He took the train to Europe and made his way to a quiet little hotel. He was just getting ready for bed when he heard a funny little noise. Looking round, he saw three young mice.

The boldest of them said to him: "Good day, big sir. Shall we have the pleasure of seeing you here for long?"

"Oh no," replied Babar. "I am only passing through. I am looking for Father Christmas."

"Looking for Father Christmas! Why, he is here, in this house! We know him well," said the little mice. "We will show you his room."

"Hurrah!" cried Babar in astonishment.
"What a piece of luck!" and he followed
them up the stairs.

The three little mice led him right up to
the attic. But what were they doing so
busily there in the corner?

"Where are you?" called Babar.

"Here," replied the little mice. "Come quickly! We have unhooked Father Christmas! Here he is! He stays quietly here all the year round. But on Christmas Day they come to fetch him to put him on the top of a brand-new Christmas tree.

"When the party is over he goes back to his corner and we can play with him."

"But this is not the one I am looking for!" said Babar. "I want to see the *real* Father Christmas, the living Father Christmas, not a doll!"

Next morning Babar wandered along the quays, deep in thought. On the stall of a second-hand bookseller he found a big book which contained some pictures of Father Christmas. He promptly bought it, and took it to his room to read.

Unfortunately the text was printed in a language he did not know.

The hotel manager kindly gave him the address of the celebrated professor, William Jones.

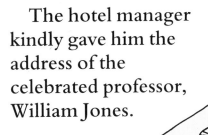

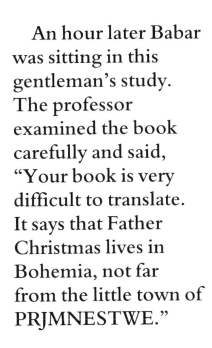

An hour later Babar was sitting in this gentleman's study. The professor examined the book carefully and said, "Your book is very difficult to translate. It says that Father Christmas lives in Bohemia, not far from the little town of PRJMNESTWE."

"But I'm afraid," said the professor, "that I cannot find any more definite information on this point."

Babar went and sat down in the park to think things over.

At that moment a little dog who was passing by said to him: "Excuse me, sir, I am

very good at finding things. If only I could smell the doll belonging to that little girl over there, I could take you to Father Christmas, for it was he who gave the doll to her. I am a stray dog, and I should be very pleased to go with you." Babar looked at the little dog and said: "Very well, I will take you with me."

Then Duck (that was the name Babar had given the dog) sniffed the doll and Babar gave him a piece of sugar.

Before leaving, Babar went back to see the wise Professor William Jones, who returned his book to him and gave him a few extra directions. It was in a forest, on a mountain, about fifteen miles from the town, that Father Christmas must live.

Babar arrived after a complicated journey at the little town of PRJMNESTWE.

It was cold and had snowed a great deal, so Babar made special preparations. He bought some skis, hired a sledge, and was driven to the foot of the mountain. Soon he had to leave the sledge, and, alone with Duck, with his skis on his feet and his knapsack heavily filled, he climbed towards the mysterious forest.

Duck was very excited. He looked round, and yelped softly. Then he lifted his tail, stood still, and sniffed. He must have recognised the smell of Father Christmas.

Suddenly Duck ran off. "I've got it! I've got it! The scent!" he cried, barking loudly, and the whole forest echoed.

But what was that moving in the wild forest? It was the little dwarfs of the mountain hiding behind the tree-trunks!

Duck wanted to go nearer and see
them, but they rushed at him and quickly
bombarded him with hard snowballs,
which landed on his head, in his eyes, and
on his body.

Half suffocated and half blinded, with
his tail between his legs, he ran quickly
back to his master. He was out of breath
and miserable.

Babar stopped when he saw him.
"Good gracious, Duck!" he said.
"Whatever has happened?" And Duck
told him of his adventure with the
little bearded dwarfs.

"Good! We must go up to them!"
replied Babar. "I am very curious to make
the acquaintance of these gnomes.
Take me to them."

When Babar met the dwarfs, they tried to bombard him, too, but Babar calmly blew on them through his trunk. They fell on top of each other and ran off without a sound. Babar burst out laughing.

But just then a violent storm broke. The wind blew so hard that the snow stung Babar's eyes and skin. He could see nothing. He struggled on desperately; then, realising that it was dangerous to go on, he decided to dig a hole and take shelter.

Next he made a roof with a stick, his skis and some blocks of snow. Now they had a little shelter. "How cold it is!" thought Babar. "My trunk is beginning to freeze!" Duck was also very tired. Suddenly Babar felt the earth give way beneath him. He and Duck disappeared. Where had they fallen?

By mistake they had fallen
through a ventilator into the
cave of Father Christmas!

"Father Christmas!" cried
Babar. "Duck, we are there!"

Then, overcome with
weariness, cold and
excitement, he fainted.

"Come, little dwarfs of the mountains," said Father Christmas, "forget your quarrel! We must undress him and warm him."

They all set to work immediately. They undressed Babar, and then rubbed him hard with spirits, using big brushes, and the dwarf doctor gave him some medicine.

Soon Babar was drinking good hot soup with Father Christmas, after thanking him from the bottom of his heart.

While being shown over Father Christmas's house, Babar explained that he had made this long journey especially

to ask him to come to his kingdom to give
toys to the little elephants as he did to the
little human children.

See note on following page.

Father Christmas was very touched by this request, but he told Babar that he could not come to the land of the elephants on Christmas Eve because he was very tired. "I had the greatest difficulty last year in arranging an even distribution of toys to all the children in the world," he added.

N.B. The visit included: the big room where Father Christmas usually lived and where Babar had fallen through the hole that you can see on the right; the toyrooms, for example: the doll room, the soldier room, the fancy-dress room, the train room, the room of building-toys, the toy animal room, the bat and ball room, etc. (all these were stored in boxes or sacks); and then the dwarfs' dormitories, the lifts and the machine-rooms.

"Oh, Father Christmas," said
Babar, "I do understand, but
you know you must look after
yourself, get more air, leave your
underground house. Come with me
now to the land of the elephants and
warm yourself in the sun. You will
be rested and better for Christmas."

Pleased by this idea, Father Christmas commanded the little dwarfs to take care of everything. Then he went away with Babar and Duck in his flying machine, F.C. No. 1.

They arrived. Father Christmas admired
the scenery. Elephants came running from
all directions to welcome him. Pom, Flora
and Alexander hurried up. Arthur
clambered on to the roof of a house so
that he could see better, and Zephir
climbed a tree.

When they were all quiet again, Queen Celeste introduced her three children to Father Christmas, as well as Arthur and Zephir. "Ah! It is you who wrote!" said Father Christmas. "I am very pleased to see you, and I can promise you a very happy Christmas."

Often Father Christmas went out riding on a zebra. Babar went with him on his bicycle. But every day Father Christmas rested for two whole hours in the sun as Doctor Capoulosse had advised him to.

Sometimes Pom, Flora and Alexander came to look at him when he was lying in his hammock, but they were very quiet so as not to disturb him.

One day Father Christmas said to Babar: "My dear friend, it will soon be Christmas, and I must go now and distribute my toys to the little human children; they are waiting for them. But I have not forgotten th promise I made to the little elephants. Do you know what I have in this sack? A real Father Christmas costume made to fit you! A magic costume that will enable you to fly through the air, and a sack that is always full of toys. You shall take my place on Christmas Eve in the land of the elephants. I promise to come back when I have finished my work, and to bring a beautiful Christmas tree for your children."

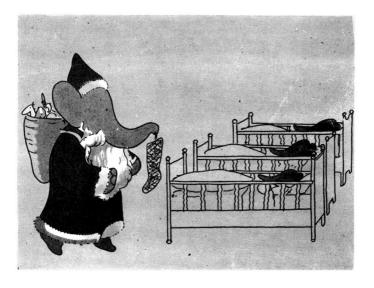

On Christmas Eve
Babar did what
Father Christmas
had told him. As
soon as he had put
on the costume and
the beard he felt
himself grow light,
and begin to fly.

"It really is
extraordinary," he
thought, "and most
useful for
distributing toys."

He made haste to
finish before dawn.

What excitement
there was in every house on Christmas
morning, when the little elephants woke
up! In the royal palace Queen Celeste
peeped through the door of the room.

Pom was emptying his stocking, Flora nursing her doll; Alexander jumped up and down on his bed shouting: "What a lovely Christmas! What a lovely Christmas!"

As he had promised, Father Christmas came back bringing with him a beautiful tree. Thanks to him, the family celebration was a great success.

Arthur and Zephir, Pom, Flora and
Alexander had never seen anything more
beautiful than the fir tree sparkling with
lights.

The next day Father Christmas flew away once more in his machine back to his underground palace and his people, the little dwarfs.

On the banks of the big lake, Babar, Celeste, Arthur, Zephir and the three children waved their handkerchiefs, a little sad at seeing their friend Father Christmas go. Happily he has promised to come back each year to the land of the elephants.

First published in Great Britain 10 October 1940 by Methuen Children's Books
A Division of Reed International Books Limited
Michelin House, 81 Fulham Road, London SW3 6RB
First published in this format 1991. Text copyright © 1991 Methuen
Children's Books. All rights reserved. Printed in France.
ISBN 0 416 16352 1